and the girl called to the moon

WHAT IS LOVE?

and the girl called to the moon

WHAT IS LOVE?

by Matt Hopwood

Illustrations by
Florence Boyd

First Published in United Kingdom 2021
in association with
Independent Publishing Network
71-75 Shelton Street, Covent Garden,
London, WC2H 9JQ, UK

ISBN 978-1-80068-128-6

British Library
Cataloguing-in-Publication-Data
A catalogue record for this book
is available from the British Library.

Typeset in Verdigris MVB
Printed and bound by J. Thompson - Glasgow
Cover Design by Giles Ellis
Cover illustration by Florence Boyd

“A gift to all those that love, especially to those with arms outstretched in the night, who having given all they had left, speak alone to what they would have loved and hearing only in reply the moon upon the water, begin to sing, hoping the real one might appear.”

Martín Prechtel - *Stealing Benefacio’s Roses*

Welcome

As I have wandered through the world talking to people about love I have fallen into stories of delight and joy, of humour and awakening. I have also been saddened to hear so many folk, both old and young, express that they have never felt love in their life. How can I love?' some have asked me as if I might have an answer. 'What is love?' others have questioned, 'I have never felt it - never felt loved'. 'Perhaps I do not deserve love' some have shared. And my answers have always drifted, caught on the winds, ephemeral, insubstantial. What I have always wanted to say is how loved they are, how I love them, though I have only just met them. How their joy is my joy, their sorrow mine too. Their liberation is my liberation. So if they have never felt loved, never felt the joys of belonging and being held, then I am equally undone. What I want is to hold their hand and be with them and comfort them. But I am shy and sometimes lack courage and so don't always do and say as I should.

So this little book is for all who struggle to love - which is all of us. Perhaps we have never felt love, cannot recognise it, do not know how to love. Maybe we feel like we don't belong, like we are strangers in a foreign land, strangers in our own skin. This little big story is me holding your hand and telling you that you belong, that you are held, that you are loved, that you are not alone.

and the girl called to the moon

WHAT IS LOVE?

First light. On the shore she waited. Fleeting memories of her fourteen years came in visions, meandering formlessly through her mind. Her body numb, her hair moving in the cool breeze of the morning light, she waited.

Something was happening but what it was she could not tell. Something was awakening in the flickering murmuring movement of her warrior heart, in the songs of the stars, in the shifting sands beneath her feet. Moving, stirring - something was beginning or ending. And all she knew was that she had to be here, to witness, to be present to what was coming to pass.

Alone, afraid, she had made her way through the night. Across sand dunes, between clumps of long marram grass swaying in the westerly breeze, she walked barefoot until she found herself on the vast shoreline looking out to the eastern horizon. Here she waited. Voices in the air, in the waters, whisperings in the light. Just beyond her reach.

After some time she closed her eyes and began to sing, a little shyly at first. A melody came to her, a distant memory of an ancient lullaby. It felt like a love song, though love was something she could not describe, had never felt. 'Am I loved? she wondered. What is love?' she whispered to herself.

•

The sun spread its light across the water gently, silently unfolding across the hills and valleys. And the sun called tenderly to the earth, 'She does not know, she has forgotten, she longs to remember but cannot find her way.'

The earth remained silent.

So the light built. Warmth touched the soil and the leaves of the trees and tips of the grasses. Light reflected on the water, illuminating the girl on the shore.

'This is my love,' whispered the sun to the earth. 'For her, for you, for all beings. In this moment I warm you, you can feel me. She can feel me. Love is this embrace.'

Then the earth slowly stirred. A low murmur of awakening. An opening of leaf, a release of pressure, the rise of energy. In the distance the call of the first bird.

'This is our love,' the earth intoned. 'I am here to honour your light and warmth and hold you when your light recedes and you disappear from sight. I am forever here to receive your embrace, your love. This is my love for you.'

'Remember my love. Remember this sweetness,' whispered the sun to the earth. 'Remember. Remember us,' she gently called to the curious girl standing alone on the shore, singing an ancient lullaby, waiting, waiting.

The light grew luminous and golden in the day, and the earth warmed and turned, and the waters rose and fell with the tides.

'This is love,' the waters called from the wild places and the gentle shores. 'We dance and break upon the land, each wave is a kiss, each ripple a caress. We hold the memory of every love that has ever existed. We have moved in every being. So we love on behalf of all. Our love is all love, our wild caress is your caress, our storms are your storms. This is our love.'

And the sun, earth and waters played in the light of day, entwined, inseparable in their love.

And the green people, the plants and nature spirits, danced and sang as they always do when they receive such love. 'This is love,' they cried out to the girl, to the earth, the waters and anyone else who might listen. 'We are given exactly what we need, just enough. We can feel the warmth of your light, the moist kiss of rains, the embrace of the earth. This is love. THIS is love.' And the trees swayed their agreement, gently moving in the breeze, stretching and bending their

forms, connecting with the stars, reaching deep into the tremulous earth.

'Let us go to her,' the water nymphs called from the shore. 'She can almost hear. She is remembering. She is singing herself home.'

White and beautiful Grandmother Moon emerged in the sky, low on the horizon.

'We must wait my darlings,' she sighed. 'For she has lost everything and from that lonely place she must find the courage to seek out love and life, to fully return home to us. Only she can find the way home. Wait my loves, wait. She is coming - she must come. She senses us, feels us. The time is now and she is remembering, she is finding her courage. Be ready my darlings, for she will need all your love and wisdom.'

Time passed.

Dusk approached and the shadows lengthened as the sun sank low in the western sky. All day long the girl had waited, singing, watching, remembering. Searching the ocean for a sign.

As the sunlight retreated the moonlight swelled casting a curious whiteness upon the land and sea, creating soft shadows of inky blackness. With the setting sun's rays upon her body, Grandmother Moon reflected her light upon the earth and all its creatures. Conversing with the trees, making pathways to the stars, she gently sang, 'I am the keeper of the past, the gateway to healing, the magnitude of my love is infinite and endures forever.'

•

In this ethereal light the girl stood, alone and uncertain on the cooling sand, before a diminishing tide. Neither tall, nor short. Young and brave, her hair hung wildly around her slender shoulders, her eyes wide and beautiful. Her heart throbbed. The song that came from her lips faltered before the waxing moon. Her breath became shallow and her body trembled

with a grief that was as old as time. It was her grief, but she felt, in that moment, that she held the grief of all people.
'Who am I?' she whispered to herself. 'I am ready to know. I am ready.'

Brought up in the hills of the western lands, she considered herself a very 'ordinary' person. And though life seemed to pass uneventfully, she was aware of a feeling deep in her stomach that she could not recognise. A fire she could not understand. Every day the feeling grew. Every day confusion fell about her like the morning dew, a thin ephemeral layer that covered her senses and clouded her vision.

She was happiest by the sea and in the dunes that lay between her home and the wide ocean. Here she would play for hours, feeling the sunlight upon her face, listening to the wind in the grass, watching the little boats move slowly across the horizon. But she was invisible to them, a warrior queen from another home, a brighter place that felt as enormous as the nights sky. She longed to be seen by another, to feel she belonged to something. Like a solitary star in the evening sky she was waiting for the vast cosmos to unfold around her.

'I am here' she called out desperately into the night sky, her eyes searching the horizon for a sign. But there was no reply. Just the gentle movement of the waves on the shore.

Then slowly, imperceptibly, a calmness settled about her. In that moment a courage and certainty grew within her. In spite of all the things she had been taught to forget, in spite of the numbness that filled her waking thoughts and actions, a spark of ancient remembrance flickered and ignited in her heart, coursing through her quivering body. She knew what she must do. So with all her passion, with all that remained of her will, vulnerable, alone but unafraid, the girl looked up and called to the moon.

'What is love? I feel alone here. I do not know what love is. Have I ever felt it, touched it? I do not know how to love. I belong to no one. Who am I? What am I? What is love?'

But the moon remained silent. The girl fell to her knees, a feather on the shores of this half-forgotten world, weeping tears of loss and remembrance, of frustration and fear.

Into this great silence spoke the earth. Beyond whispers now, beyond doubt, the girl heard her voice. It resonated across the hills and dunes and trembled the ground beneath her feet.

'When you walk my child, walk gently on me, as though barefoot. Make each step an embrace, each touch a caress. Hold me as you would hold your dearest friend. Defend me from harm, sit quietly by my side and know our being together is enough. I will always hold you and will never leave you. I am always here for you. I wait for you everyday and through each night. Come home to me. This is my love for you.'

In the gloaming, with darkness descending all about, the girl sat on the shimmering sands of the shore and cried. 'But there is darkness and pain and forgetfulness all around me. I long to love, to live, but this feels overwhelming.'

The wind rose then, a soft breeze upon the land, encircling the girl, lifting her curly hair till it moved and glistened in the light of the full moon. 'This is love' the wind whispered. 'I am your sister and though you cannot see me I am always with you. I offer life and breath to you and shape your body so you can feel all the edges of your being. Be with me now my love. There is no need to fear. I am here, you are here, feel my touch. We are companions in this moment; in this darkness, you are found.'

The girl and the wind remained together, invisible to each other, close and intimate.

Above her in the night sky Grandmother Moon shone her light brilliantly across the surface of the land. 'For this reason you were born my love, for this moment now.' She laughed. 'You are a tiny glowing speck in this vast cosmos: a firefly in the night. I shine my light on you so you may know this love. For in this infinite space of creation you are a beautiful part. Small, obscure, perfect, my light finds you just as you are. You are part of a whole my love, not lost but forever found.

Look up. I am here. The whole cosmos stands before you. The earth holds you as mother, the wind encircles you as sister, and I am here as grandmother to love you and show you balance and the connection between all things.
Love is here within you and without. You are a part of its vastness.'

'How do I begin to love?' asked the girl, the words tumbling from her as if in a dream.

'Come to me,' spoke the sea.

'Come' whispered a thousand sea sprites, riding on the waves. 'Come to her. For she is the keeper of all our memories. All joys, loves, pains and hurts reside in her. Not one being on this earth has loved, lost, found or hurt without her presence. Come to her now and forever after.'

'Swim in my waters' said the sea. 'Whisper words of love to me, ease my memories, share my sorrows and my joys. With each word you heal everything and everyone.

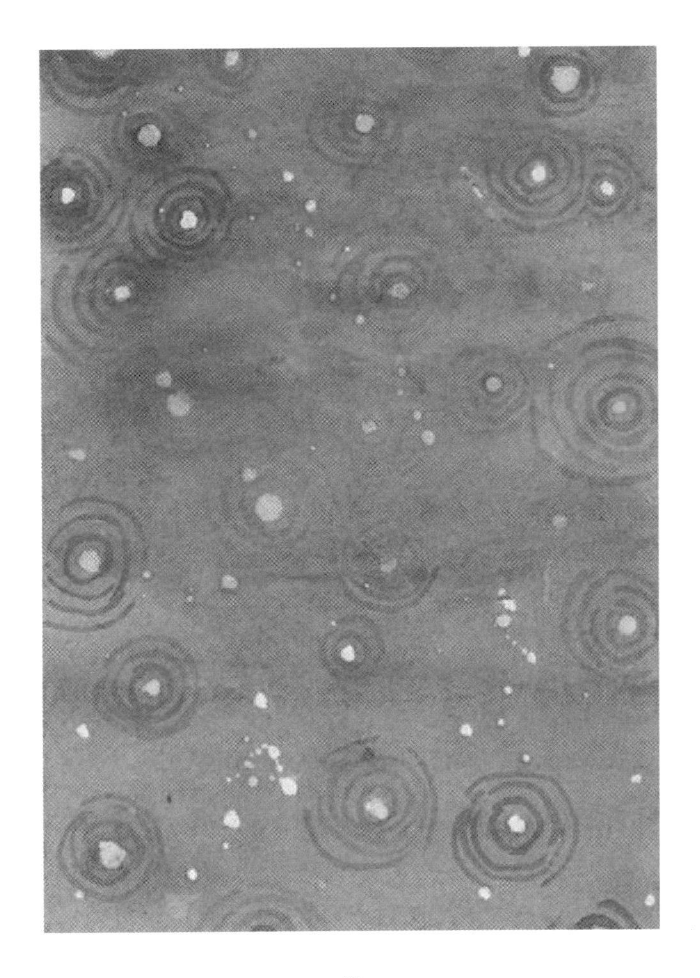

With each gesture of kindness you move more deeply into love. Through me you can love the whole cosmos and everything in it. Come to me. This is how you begin.'

Then the waters swelled and the sea rose covering the girl in her cool embrace. 'I love you - you are never lost,' she sang. 'I am you, you are me. Let go, let go my love for I will NEVER leave you.'

Laughter filled the night then, the girl joyful in the wild ecstatic moment.

Found and unafraid.

‘So this is love’ said the girl, ‘I remember this feeling from long ago. But I feel such fire burning inside me still and pain and anger. Is this love too?’

Into the moonlit darkness came the first flickers of morning light, the softening of blacks to greys and blues, and then a piercing ray of sunlight exploded across the seascape.

‘Fire is love too,’ wailed the sun. ‘Fire inside, pain and hurt, they are love. I warm the earth each day, I lay my fire upon the surface, and sometimes it scorches the earth whom I love best. And it burns. Love is not perfect, love encompasses all things. Love is a way of being, an intention that you set before you as a beam of light to bring warmth to another, to bring life. This is love.’

The girl sat motionless on the sand. Calm and unafraid.

‘I want to love, to feel alive. If I cannot love, I cannot live.’ She spoke, certain now before the rising sun.

'It is time,' whispered a thousand sea sprites dancing on the waves, sparkling in the light of the dawn. Let us begin. Come now, come. You are ready.'

'Come' sighed Grandmother Moon as she surrendered to the light of the dawning sun.

'Come now' whispered the sea. 'It is time.'

The girl rose then and looked out on the vast ocean that stretched before her and the thousand points of light that danced upon the surface. Taking off her shoes she moved barefoot and gently across the sand. Kneeling at the shoreline she whispered words of love to the sea, allowing the waters to run across her hands.

In the east the sun rose and the west made a home for the moon. And she smiled and lowered her head to each in turn, in gratitude and wonder. And the wind moved about her, whispering softly softly, 'This is love - this is enough.'

Epilogue

We all sit by the shore sometimes, as the girl in this book does, longing to belong, yearning to be loved. Never forget how perfect you are, how loved. You were made for this moment, that is why you are here. You are needed now more than you know, your feeling searching heart is needed, beneath this sun, on this beloved world, spinning through the infinite cosmos.

A Little Big Story

Whilst this is a simple story, a little story about a young girl, it is also a big story, because the girl could be anyone of us and the shore she stands by could be our front door, the fields near our home or the city streets where we live. Her experience could be our experience and her bravery and courage ours too.

It is no small thing to stop and breathe and wonder what this extraordinary existence might be about. Why am I here? Why do I feel alone? How can I truly belong? What is love?

To offer love and gratitude is no small thing either. To sit alongside 'all that is,' to honour the earth and the sea, these are acts of radical kindness, of courage, and they can change the world. They CAN change the world.

To see yourself as part of the fabric of the cosmos and to honour that seeing. To offer love and gratitude, prayers, flowers, smoke, in whichever way resonates for you, is a rebellious act. It defies most of popular culture, it is statement of intent: I am only the sum of all our parts - my love is bound up with yours and my liberation too.

Matt Hopwood

Matt Hopwood is an Author, Speaker and Sound Healer. In 2012 he launched the project A Human Love Story that has seen him walk thousands of miles around the UK and journey around the world creating deep sharing spaces where people can feel held, share their human stories and be heard. These stories have culminated in two published books and an online audio collection. Through these sharings Matt hopes to help nurture understanding, love and compassion across communities and cultures. Featured on BBC Radio 2 & 4 on numerous occasions and in journals in the US, Matt's work explores listening as a transformative tool for change. This naturally evolved into working as a Sound Healing Practitioner with the College of Sound Healing.

Florence Boyd

Florence's practice shifts between the figurative and the abstract. Finding and unearthing connections links a lot of her work both visually as an illustrator and collaboratively. She is based in Wales and draws a lot of inspiration from the beautiful landscape of the South Coast.